I have cultivated my hysteria with pleasure and terror.

~ Charles Baudelaire

Also by Matthew Jose

Of Drink And Greatness
Long Odds at Best (Silver Bow Publishing)
Depending Upon The Muse
Even The Flowers Mock Me

And writing as DOUBLE TROUBLE Jose& James

Double Trouble Vol. I – Poems from the Edge
Double Trouble Vol. II – Deviate the Levitate
Double Trouble Vol. II – Poemetrics
Double Trouble Vol IV – The Obsession

Chronicles from the Periphery

by:

Matthew Jose

720 Sixth Street, Box # 5
New Westminster, BC
CANADA V3L3C5

Title: CHRONICLES FROM THE PERIPHERY
Author: Matthew Jose
Cover Design: Kayla Jose
Editor: Candice james
© 2020 Silver Bow Publishing
ISBN 9781774030684 (softcover)
ISBN 97817740309691 (e-book)

Library and Archives Canada Cataloguing in Publication

Title: Chronicles from the periphery / by Matthew Jose.
Names: Jose, Matthew, 1976- author.
Description: Poems.
Identifiers: Canadiana (print) 20200180517 | Canadiana (ebook) 20200180525 | ISBN 9781774030684 (softcover) | ISBN 9781774030691 (HTML)
Classification: LCC PS3610.O75 C47 2020 | DDC 811/.6—dc23

5

Dedicated to poor life choices

Chronicles from the Periphery

CONTENTS

Chronicles from the Periphery

The Poet

The poet must sing a thousand songs
before dying a thousand deaths.
A thousand symphonies soft, the music must play on.
Long after a human will is broken beyond repair.
Long after the voices have all been tucked away.
Long after a ship is lost at sea.

The poet must sink to a thousand ocean bottoms.
When the voice in your head says the hell with it, fight.
When the marrow in your bones says the hell with it, fight.
When the depths of your soul screams the hell with it, fight.

For this is when it finally reveals.

Harkened Voices

Confused, dizzy and brimming with madness
I step into a shower
with water too hot and a nubbin of soap too small.
Sure, I've broken some hearts
but this hardly seems the right time
to discuss such misgivings.

What ever would we do without our beautiful lies?

A voice, harkened and thread-sewn, asks
if I would like her company in the bath,
and her company is far better
than room temperature gravy
so. I say yes with an outpouring of myself,
thinking *this sure beats feeling as good as the next guy.*

Willow Weep

If I put 4 on the 6 will the willow weep for me?
With nostalgia at bay, the hard work is done early
and unknowingly.

The realization that I am old is painless
unlike the act of being old itself.

I no longer average 20 and 10 a night.
I'm not sure how old Burroughs was when he shot his wife
but I can be sure his realization came a fraction too late.

Bukowski said there's nothing worse than too late.
I tend to think Burroughs would have agreed.

Lollipops and Mediocrity

Spider bites and common pains.
Lollipops and mediocrity.
Turning frozen water to melting wax.
Neither chosen nor welcomed.

I lay here this evening, expressionless,
my famished mind considering these
and other swarming thoughts.

Having died so many times already
I am sure the final death will be no different.
I can only hope it is peaceful.
I can only hope it is mild.
To be ready is to not wait for its arrival.

Sun Bleached

If I write a little each day
I feel good amidst the turmoil.
If I drink a little each day
I feel good amidst the turmoil.

When I don't do these two things
I become like a wheelbarrow gathering rain
or a well past his prime soprano
singing off key notes through chipped teeth.

You see, tangled souls can't be straightened,
but with time and wisdom gained
they can become less marred by the bulge.

If you've ever seen a starfish washed ashore,
sun bleached and abandoned,
then you would know this already.

Time is the master.
Time cleanses us all.

Only a Sip

Reluctant emergings
come to rid and cleanse and remind me
that there was never any real need to begin with.

It's all just for the good of the game,
the Broadway show we all live each day.

The world is the stage.
We are the players.
And it's a hell of a fun game to play
once you peek through the curtain.

So let us all consolidate and be easy on the journey.
It's such a short time we must endure indeed.

Downwardly Mobile

I shake the piss dribbles off as I finish and walk to the sink.
Not to wash my hands but because I notice there is hair
all over and the toothpaste cap has gone missing again.

I look into the mirror.
I consider the moment.

What's the point of screaming loudest
in a room full of screaming faces?

I pick a piece of blueberry out
from between my two front teeth.
Then walk out of the bathroom looking forward to
a downwardly mobile afternoon.

Hold the Handle

It's 7:00 in the morning and I've already been up for 3 hours.
7:06 to be exact.
And I'm straddling the line of sanity and insanity.
Must have been one of those nights again.

Sitting here on the toilet I begin to think.
I've always lived at places where you have to stand there
and hold the handle down when you flush after handling your
business.
Otherwise you only get a partial removal of excrement.

Therefore, it's been my good fortune
to see many a bowel movement
endure its eminent downward spiral,
whisked away to some far-off land.

I used to wonder where all the poop goes.
I think I asked somebody when I was a kid.
I don't remember the answer.
I guess I must have stopped wondering at some point.
I've also always seen the symbolism in everything.

Even nothing can hold meaning
 if you read into it deep enough.
I've had the good fortune
to read into many a bowel movement.
Each one has meant something different.
Each one has meant something special to me.

His Echo

Co-existing fantasies and denied realities
dance a dominance tango, for it takes two;
the oddness of life.

The disappearance of an eye mask.
The allure of expectation and disappointment.
Fine companions.

She slithered in, harmonizing with his echo.
It was with his guard down
that he noticed the branch shake
as she gently plucked the not yet ripened fruit from the tree.

Shots

One shot.
Two shots.
Three shots.
Four.
I'm starting to feel good, but I think I need more.

Five shots.
Six shots.
Seven shots.
Eight.
Before I felt good but now, I feel great.

Nine shots.
Ten shots.
Eleven shots.
Twelve.
Headfirst into the abyss, shall we delve?

Constant Change

The only constant is change,
and I've been known to change
from time to time.

When I was young, I knew very little.
As I grew older, I knew even less.

As I've become much older, I realize
there was never anything to know in the first place.

The tree of wisdom
now shade covers and comforts me
as I lie beneath its foliaged umbrella.

Hangover

I was hanging out with my hangover the other day
and it suddenly dawned on me,
I have never had money, but I have always had beer.
At the end of the day I am going to call this a victory,
small one as it may be, a victory, nonetheless.
I then realized that my life
vaguely resembles that of a man ice fishing in Miami.

Dear Postal Service,
From here on in please forward all mail to my new address:

Rock Bottom, USA
Thank you in advance.
Sincerely,
Proud Bottom Dweller

Aren't We All?

Lacing a hangover with black coffee dignity,
like touching the gum stuck under a handrail
and being able to laugh about it,
I go to my car to change a tire that isn't even flat.

Thinking about something comical like death and dying
or overly aggressive wiping after taking a crap
or hoisting erections at inopportune times,
I suddenly remember a neighbor I used to have
who took up collecting dead insect specimens
upon receiving his terminal diagnosis.

Maybe being surrounded by dead things
helped him deal with the process.

Maybe he was just strange and dying.

Aren't we all?

Additions and Subtractions

He was a writer too and his was a slow suicide;
that of a man emotionally bankrupt.
He realized that the things we can't change,
in time, may change us.
But he was also bankrupt of patience.
Time sure does take its toll.

Throughout his life he had seen people
be unbelievably cruel to each other
and for some reason it hurt him deeply to see this.
Probably hurt him more than it hurt the average person.
He had also seen the incredible beauty and kindness
with which people treat each other on occasion as well;
in hindsight that's probably what kept him around
for as long as he ended up staying.

He saw the world as a place where selling sin was easy.
Selling God was easy.
But selling the truth was damn near impossible.

He couldn't stand that this truth gnawed at him,
but he couldn't deny the fact that it did either.
He would carry his manuscript everywhere he went,
always making changes.
Additions.
Subtractions.
Corrections.
I guess in the end he figured he could never quite get it
to where he wanted it to be, never quite right.
The note found by his body read:
"I now know how the story ends."

Decency

I was reading the newspaper a couple days ago
and came across something I found interesting.

A classified advertisement read as such.
Wanted: a little decency in a cruel world.

As far as I know there has yet to be a response.

She Can't

Her lips taste like melancholy
and easy Sunday mornings.
I like that about her most.
I have no desire to know
the inner workings of the whole thing,
it's enough to enjoy her flavors.

Many times I've wondered
if she could talk to me about Hank Mobley.
Or Clifford Brown.
Or Dexter Morgan.
Or anything real.

But I know she can't.
So I let it go.

Why ruin a perfect thing?

Dangerous Instruments

It's the dirty socks and other dangerous instruments
like sharp rocks that always find their way into my shoes.
They're keeping me sloppy.
They're keeping me hardened.

But those same sharp stones find my soul spaces as well
and it's the neatest of miracles.
They cut, these shards, so deep and so perfect,
like swallowing the light within,
and I know it's killing me and I'm laughing all the while.

This wreckage is all part of the stew,
along with pigeon holes and fountains of youth,
and I say count me in for a double portion.

I had a dream just last night that I won the lottery
but chose to starve to death to prove some kind of point.
I don't remember what point I was trying to prove
but I remember feeling the actual hunger pangs
in my sleep.

This morning I woke up as broke and poor
as I was when I went to sleep
but without any moral convictions prohibiting breakfast
so I made a couple fried eggs and drank a beer.

Clearly the makings of a great day.

Ancient Rhythms

The many moods of the lotus cross my mind
as I sit in an Adirondack chair
watching red and blue birds feed
and thunderstorms approach.

Those birds have no idea
that I've been ground up and revived yet again,
but I feel somehow their birdsongs
are meant just for me today.

These ancient rhythms will become my cargo
as I go on, feeling invigorated
by the onset of the misty oneness.

Just another starting point.
Just another road.

What Do You Mean You Don't Drink?

I'm in a hot shower on a cold winter morning
in an apartment where the heat works on occasion at best.
Outside the blinding check engine light in my car
is the least of my concerns.
My dashboard stays lit up like the fourth of July.

And an onslaught of phone calls from debt collectors
allows me to feel like Mr. Popular.
I often ask the unsympathetic voices on the other end of the receiver
when they first realized that they too had lost their soul.
I often hear a dial tone in response.

I've always found money for booze though,
it seems folks like me always do.
It's a modern miracle of financial planning really.
A nipper is a dollar these days, for the cheap stuff.
It's still 80 proof. Taste is a secondary consideration.
My favorite liquor store sells red wine for three bucks a bottle.
I buy five at a time. That usually lasts me a day and a half.
I love running out of drink around dusk.
The walk back to the store gives me a flash of purpose,
although fleeting.
The owner of that liquor store often tells me he never drinks.
Says he can't stand the stuff.

My favorite moments in life are the ironic ones.
Every once in a long while the liquor store owner
throws in a cheap dollar nipper for free,
doing so in sweeping dramatic fashion
to ensure I'm quite aware of the benevolent act.
What's funny is I've never expected any freebies from life.
I enjoy paying my dues; it gives me another flash of purpose.

> *"What do you mean you don't drink?"*
I say this into the mirror before my first sip of each day.
I get no response.

Tip the Scale

She's like a hot curling iron born of transformation,
luckily I don't wear hats.
She offers me a handful of keys
and a mouthful of sorrow
and I take whatever she is willing to give.
She causes my pen's effortless movements at time
and guides me through the vacant snores.

She is the grain of sand that finally tips the scale.
She even puts toothpicks in the cocktail weenies.

She is my kind of class.
She is my kind of way.

She is all of this and so much more.

What's the Point?

Enduring the shellfire.
Understanding the futility.
Resting upon the sparrows nesting places.

And all the while the taste of the good stuff
is hardly different than
the taste of a burnt down mermaid's tail.
But there is a strange warmth to be felt
in the ember's remains.

And even beginnings have their own starting point.
Choppy, mended and glued.
Is it all truly without meaning?

Melancholy Muse

Feeling a darker shade of blue,
I sit here watching a candle flame flicker and dance.
The flame is like a ballerina
with a pension and flare for the dramatic.
     Seductive.
     Smooth.
     Easy.

Imploring the necessary life accessories.
     Like anger.
     Like restlessness.
     Like my melancholy muse.
     Like lumps of vacancy.

Dull and endless and gradually growing.
Feeling a darker shade of blue,
I sit here unable to go forward
and unable to go back.

Strange

Mingling in the mystified.
Clamoring through the smoke screens.
Simply asking forgiveness for belonging.

Like flashes of lightning.
Or bayonets and eye gouges.
We all just want a chance to squeeze the produce
before we purchase it.

Cowering in the invisible.
Stampeding through the maddening windfalls.
Simply begging to stay longer than a couple minutes.

Like hard to find parking spots.
Or the dinosaur's reign.
We all just want to cut through the static.

Riptide

We can sit quietly upon mountain tops
and stare at vast spaces,
but we will never truly understand just how big it all is.

We can pass through this life
without so much as a whisper,
but we will never truly understand the silence
of the unknown.

We can peek under the edges
or fly high toward the sun,
but we will never truly touch the swaying sky.

And like the roaches climbing the asylum walls.
Or the ramblings within those same asylums.
It's of no use to fight against the riptide.

Momentary Immortality

A nothing man works nothing words into a nothing poem
about nothing much at all.

This life is so strange,
the time melting into these books
like knocking berries off vines,
flanked by uselessness and triviality.

It's the spider webbed dance we all take part in
knowing full well the thing is going to get us anyhow.

Maybe the word fire has gone out.
Maybe it was never there.

It's a kick to the teeth.
Preferable to a kick to the balls?
I would settle for both if it meant momentary immortality.

Conundrum

It's only when I'm not drinking that I want a drink.
Conundrum, right?
I'm so good at drinking.
My expertise is obvious to all who know me,
and even to those who don't
.

I strongly believe that beverage imbibing
should be an Olympic event.
I would proudly don the stars and stripes
and pick up pints
while carrying the torch for my country.
What would my uniform look like?
Spandex?
A tight fitting unitard?
Lord knows I've been training hard for years
 for this opportunity.

Would my country be as proud of me
as they are of gymnasts?
As proud as they are of the gold medal fencing champion?
The rifleman on skis?

Would I be expected to stand on the podium
for the medal ceremony?
What if I stumble as I walk to accept my great honor?
What if I mumble and slur my speech
as I speak on behalf of America?
Would I be tested for performance enhancing substances?

Perhaps nothing would be expected of me
except to be a damn good drunk.

Dear mom, I have found my niche!
I finally know what I want to be when I grow up.

I Wish I Were a Cat

Cats sleep a lot.
Up to 20 hours a day I've been told.
I love to sleep.
I wish I were a cat.

Cats expect to have food on their plate at all times.
They can eat all day I've been told.
I love to eat.
I wish I were a cat.

Cats poop a lot.
Multiple times a day I've been told.
I love a good bowel movement.
I wish I were a cat.

They also love the fresh air.
They love the serenity of a window sill
as they watch the world slowly pass them by, I've been told.
I love to breathe it all in.
I wish I were a cat.

Cats perch themselves
on all sorts of high places in homes.
They rest on top of cabinets and shower doors I've been told.

Sadly, I'm afraid of heights.
So much for wishing I were a cat.

Nothing Kisses

I'm trying to head south
but I'm on a cut-rate northbound train
looking out unfamiliar windows through saltwater eyes.

She packed me two banana sandwiches
and sent me on my way
with a few kisses behind the ear
that meant nothing of course.

The wind carries the seed far and wide
and I know not where I'm headed.

Shame be damned,
I'm thinking I won't last without her
as I hunker down for the longest of long nights.

It's enough to make a man set himself on fire.
But I ran through the last of my matches
waiting at the station.

Cats and String

The smaller works may simply bear a ghastly likeness,
strong enough to stand firm and close enough to smell it.
This thought has been nibbling at my eternal edges lately,
filling up all my blind spots.
      The poem.
      The words.
      The meanings.
      All worn smooth.

So much to be said for and in the lines,
with meaning wound betwixt and between.

This poem you're reading now
is just a floundering shot in the dark.

It's like we're all just cats chasing string.

Ramblings

I kept on with my ramblings, rantings and ravings i
n that tattered notebook.
Wine stained.

And all the while the universe kept expanding.
And gravity kept tugging at my marbles.
I'd open up to a random page
on the mornings I woke up foggy.
I'd see a few jotted notions.
"Beware of the one-eyed tree frog,
beware the waning fear"
That would be one.

Another was "blackouts marked by knee scrapes"
Also "This ice pick of a day
is already ramming its steel into my gut."

I wouldn't remember writing these things
but I'd like what I read.

Then I'd close the notebook and wander out,
back to that weather beaten, wooden rowboat graveyard.
I usually had the morning shift in those days.

Willingly

With fondness I drink.
In quicksand I sink.
Willingly wasting away.

With abandon of reckless.
Liquor's my temptress.
Willingly I'm led astray.

With boredom's malaise.
To a cordial I sway.
Willingly putting pause on the day.

With each sip I'm reborn.
to the madness of the storm.
Willingly I watch my mind decay.

Disheveled Ravings

Standing in my kitchen eating hot pretzels
with cold mustard,
but at least it's yellow and not Dijon,
and the stainless steel is shining that much brighter
after the cloth wash.

For some reason I suddenly remember
that Charlie Parker loved to eat chicken
so much they called him Bird.
But that's neither here nor there.

And then for some other reason I remember
what's on my agenda today:
the chore of telling my woman I no longer love her.

The dread of the chore is hanging over me
like a sack of elephants
as I see the mustard has dripped
onto my brand-new shirt.

This is clearly just the beginning
of the disheveled ravings to come today.

A Man Alone

A man alone must walk his path in life.

     Insignificant.

Alone amongst the billions of lost souls.
Alone amongst the billions of years history.
Alone amongst the billions of stories never told.

A man alone must decide if he can accept his place
in this human tragedy.

     Insignificant.

A place where a man is mourned
for approximately 48 hours after his passing.
Perhaps a wallet sized photo
magnetically adhered to a refrigerator he will become,
to be remembered
when thirst or hunger besets those left behind.

A man alone am I.
Putting pen to paper.
Crafting the word along the way.

     Insignificantly.

Forgiven Again?

She said she forgave me, but I knew better.
We spent the rest of the night
talking too much about too little
until the last stick glowing in the fire cut out.

I caught my mind sweeping through the cloudscape,
stumbling around drinking the wayward remains
of bottles and cans,
leaving filth in my wake.

She went up to bed before me.
She always did.

I wouldn't want to be the last thing I saw
before falling asleep either.

Looming

Laughing at the Styrofoam cup that's just been crushed
by the angry fist of a madman who's dressed to the nines
and flaunting a neatly knotted necktie,
I realize there is very little standing between any one of us
and the threshold of insanity.

We are all moles and misfits
in some corners and some ways of our cracked minds.

It's only a matter of time for us all really.

The permanent escape hatch looms without partiality.
Oh, to be the chosen ones!

Original

The frogs will begin dancing more in the dwindling years
for even the sun will fade away one day.
I now find myself lost in the turnip patch,
left with only madness and something to drink,
and I'm going out with the tide,
floating toward my deathbed.

It has been beautiful at times.
Perfect even.

It has been horrific at times.
Hellish even.

But the bad times don't last; neither do the good times.

I won't miss morning alarms,
 traffic jams, hangnails or the flu.
But I will miss the sound of the waves crashing.
And I will miss you.

Strangely Empty

Empty bottles.
Stacks of books.
Sitting on golden doorsteps, long ignored,
with our noses to close to our mirrors to see.

Too close to our televisions.
Our computer.
Our telephones.

Overexposure has us all strangely lost
and wading in the same sickness
like some kind of diseased feeding frenzy.

Vanishing points and a can of beans.
Get stinko and write some nonsensical chatterings.

It matters not.
Nobody is listening anyway.

Where Art Thou?

It's somewhere between
when I woke up this morning and noon,
and I need a drink as I wait in these spaces
that don't seem to be to be filled.
But my glass can be filled.
And it can also be flicked.
And it can be rocked.
And it can be shaken.
And it can be stirred
until the feeling of lightening and fire
come back to the bones.

Slow sips of the well-honed blood sauce
helps to get a few wrinkles taken out anyway.
Nothing is more tragic and delicious
than these slow days under yellow lights
knowing I have given it the hardest row I could.

I Sure Hope My Shoelaces Don't Break

Red deaths and barbarity
have me chopped to fine bits this morning.
It's a good day when the car starts
but today the engine won't turn over
and I'm reminded longshots don't often come in.

I'll spend the day shaking invisible hands
or sitting on my palms or flopping about gnawed and waving.

I'm inches from weeping
and the flies are swarming the streets.
I sure hope my shoelaces don't break when I go to tie them.
I've been told that's what sends a man to the madhouse.

Out to Sea

Some grow happy.
Some grow fat.

Some toil the soil of madness within.
Some grow untouched by the externals.

Some grow lumps and biopsied lesions.
Some simply lose their way before they even begin.

Some grow confused.
Some grow desperate.

And we all grow older
in anticipation of the hurricane
that has already gone out to sea.

Grandiose

I've been doling out some soft-boiled sentences as of late,
but now it's time to chew the thing
back down to the raw meat
and pump it full of butter and lucky midnights.

I know I'm whining to the choir
but where has all the clever stricken,
golden hued word fire gone?
The guts and beastly bellies?
The explosive ends?

Everything seems small, limp and offhand these days.
Are we all too weather battered, listless and punchy
to remember the frantic firsts?
The roaring outs and soiled courage?
The self-destructive incessancy?

Well, today I'm eating the spaghetti-o's straight out the can
and gripping what remains of the flame.
Today I'm made alive again.

Are You for Real?

It's harder to level off and piss all over these pages
when the clouds are riding low and dark
and wishing me plenty.

Maneuvering these haphazard soul bits
and battered stumbling's in the spider's lament,
like weathering the swells,
is equal parts ego and self-doubt
and it's only one of a thousand ways it kills a man.
There is a prize.
There is a price.
There is pain.
There is towel weeping.
There is blood tasting and other flavorful imperfections.

Sure it's a difficult tread.
But a necessary one.
For me.

Roll the Dice

He rushes to the Post Office.
No time to waste, it's Saturday at 11:55
and they close in 5 minutes.
Two packages to mail.
One for his wife.
One for his girlfriend.

He makes it to the counter just in time, parcels in tow.
The postal clerk asks, "How can I help you?"
He freezes with terror.
Did he put the correct gift paired with the correct card
in the correct box?
Both boxes are sealed and addressed.
The reality of the situation takes on a death grip.
The gravity of the situation weighs on him like an elephant
content with resting on his chest with nowhere to go.
He remains frozen in terror as the clerk asks again
(but this time with a perturbed voice) "how can I help you?"
The line is growing behind him.
The patience within those standing in that line behind him
is becoming emaciated.
Toes tap.
They tap faster.
They tap harder.
They tap louder.

He continues to weigh his options silently.
The little hamster in his mind
is working that wheel something fierce.
Too much to handle.
Too much pressure.

He decides to roll the dice and says,
"I will send these both via priority mail please".

Trap Snare

The space between sick and ill is partial to the formless
and when a good line hits my wet brain
I become alive for the moment.

A poet is only as good as his next poem
because the house next door is being built on stilted poesy.

Try not to forget your errors,
your one million imperfections.
Less the trap snare swift.
We all get caught sometimes.

Music of the Moon

The hours are heavy and the hard rains are falling,
these beastly breaths rest tenuous and dangling still.
I lay here this day, raw with not knowing,
taking in the shapes of it all.

The door has its shape and the windows theirs too.
And our love had a shape all its own.
But the whole thing sunk.
Guess we couldn't get the grit out after all.

Too fancy?
Too much?
Too little?
Wrong sources?
All of the above?
Fuck it.
Who cares?
She's gone.

It All Matters

He was probably one of the least intelligent people
in any of the rooms he entered.
He accepted that notion gracefully.
He never put on airs.
Never claimed to be too much, never more than he was.
In fact, he made it a point to point out how little he knew.

But he had something that mattered.
A passion to learn.
About anything.
About everything.
It all fascinated him.
Facts.
Opinions.
People's faces.
The way they dressed.
The way they moved their hands when they spoke.
The way they styled their hair so deliberately.
He wanted to hear their stories.
Every single person he met mattered to him.
He made them the most important person
in any given moment.
And they all felt it.
It's probably the reason they accepted him.
Most of them anyway.

He was often told he had an endearing quality,
the likes of which they had rarely known.
He would laugh and brush it off.
He was skilled at deflecting compliments.
They were outside his comfort zone.

Life was outside his comfort zone.

Young Versus Old

The penetrating quiet of 4 a.m. is right enough for me.
The too hot coffee, burnt tongue singe,
is felt most acutely in the spaces between my toes
and I'm still deciding if it's better to be young and unknown
versus old, known and used up.

I'm neither.
I know that.

But it's just something to consider
while the quiet persists.

Parallel Narratives

In life my contented moments
have been bookended by agonies
and at times I could not differentiate between the two.
Many nights have been spent drinking to life
and drinking to death,
paying for the privilege of the dream and the nightmare.
These parallel narratives often offered no real resolution,
rather they would devolve into conquests of dimensionality,
loosely based on non-sensical self-entertainments.

During these strange and desperate times
I would have done just about anything
to loosen the keys and rattle the brain.

And then the kindness finally came to me
and I began tucking away the wasted panic,
but never thinking about why.
Just allowing.
And slowly my best parts ended up on paper
far away from where the insanity festers.

Profound Simplicity

Walking out into the teardrops of the night,
ripened in the midst of a profound simplicity
both explorative and stabilizing,
it's easy to see why even the dolphins are dancing.

I sometimes feel like I know something.
Something that no one else can know.
In these moments I can see amazement and beauty
in even the most pedestrian of things.
What a pleasant numbness.
What a wonderful strange.

I remember one time standing there, sober as a newborn,
and the whole of everything began spinning.
And I could hear every birdsong so clearly.
It was as if the wind had become one with the sounds.
And there was the smell of grandness in the air.

Then a feeling of falling took me over.
But a falling with no fear or concern of ever landing.
I breathed in deep in that moment
thinking it could be the precursor to the final stage.

And I lifted my glass to eternity.
Just as I am tonight.

He Wasn't It

Heavy walking like floating,
into available spaces on darkening evenings,
knowing when the time is right to ignore life altogether.
Better is sometimes less; and less is sometimes more.

And I lay slowly grown whirling in the general weathers.
To soon awaken.
Perhaps senseless.
Perhaps superfluous.
But always something to remind me of the end.

Untroubled Faces

With heaping handfuls of sleeping pills
other non-solutions,
I'm all torn apart searching for a golden line or two.
There's nothing new to say.
There's nothing else to say.
It's all been said before.
Long since gone are the untainted piss-holes.

I'm just a quarter talent scratch artist
climbing scorched backyard fences,
with a satisfied, twisted look of gargled insanity.

The insults fly and they charm me plenty
like throbbing sparks
and other overlooked inconsistencies.

I hear the ticking of the flames, large and formless,
knowing the bare things are short sellers
to be warmed up through the belly
and sent straight into their hell spaces,
cooked up nicely for their untroubled faces.

Dew Moistened

Sitting here plucking each other's feathers.
Drinking through the centuries to time eternal.
Stroked by a touch soft as cement.
Thinking thoughts in a dew moistened brain.

Thoughts like...
There are times I can smell my own ass.
And my breath is of a discarded angry gristle mound.
Or my writing has too much starch
and my underwear has too many holes.

All this because our forefathers
were censored and raided.

All this to dull the senses.
All this because critics need jobs too.
All this to create poems immortal.

Because I Can

Sometimes you gotta just piss in the kitchen sink.
When I say gotta, I mean it just feels good.
Liberating.
One of those "because I can" moments in life.
Like having a beer and a shot for breakfast
on your day off work.

One of the best buzzes you will ever have
is right when you wake up,
first thing in the morning buzz.
There is a clarity it brings along with it.
It will always be one of my favorite things in life.
That, and John Coltrane.
And Bacon.
And the sound of a record album
when it's finished playing a side
and keeps spinning round and round.

It's like my life.
Good rhythm.
But stuck.
Thwack.
Thwack.
Thwack.
Thwack.

Good Bad and Ugly with Love

Dear Kay,
So many people say, "I don't even know where to start."
But I do. You are different than the rest.
I felt that immediately. I just knew it.
But I wasn't supposed to.
But I did anyway.
And I fought it, baby.
I fought it hard. And "it" won.
Knocked me right out.
It didn't even matter that I had my guard up.
Knocked me right out for real.
I never stood a chance.
Thank God! I could finally be myself.
My good, my bad, my ugly. You loved it all.
Why? I may never understand the why.

I told you I hated the "whys" of life.
You agreed. That made me love you even more.
More than I thought was humanly possible.
More than I thought I would ever allow myself to love.
More than I thought I could ever allow myself to love.
But it worked. And it was. Why me?
Why am I so lucky? Oh yeah, enough of the why's.
Stop questioning so I can start enjoying.
So much time wasted questioning.
No more. Just feel it. Reciprocate.
I promise baby, I'll be healthy one day.
I'll make you proud of me. Empty promises? Maybe.
You said it doesn't matter.
That made me love you even more.
I love you the best way I can, the only way I know how.
And you told me that was enough.
And if it ever isn't enough anymore
just know I gave you all I had.
My Good. My Bad. My Ugly.
And you took it all baby.

Bukowskian Landscapes

The dirty action doesn't always have a chance to get clean
by the time you hit the pavement.
So many of my nights have been spent in the vile places
where people gravitate
toward the type that always buys the liquor.
But I never minded that.

I spent the money knowing the sea would still roll back in.
Better than spending it on the lady fortune teller
who gave me a complex waiting for the good and the bad
that never happened.

Pass the bottles around my friends,
and scream in silence and tug at your hair!

Life is painful but temporary,
like the bite marks of an angry toddler,
so make tonight the night we shit on graves
and breathe in all the Bukowskian landscapes,
depraved in their perfection.

Baby Spoon Fed

A desperation hotter than Death Valley in July
clings to the air here and my insides
are all stoved-up and burning.
Everything feels like some grand waiting game.

Three new rejections came my way today
and I'm tip toeing ever closer to the sun,
feeling beaten by the years.
I also haven't had a good night's sleep in weeks
and the notebook is dying of starvation.

The walls are falling.
The grease is drying.
And the foundation is crumbling beneath my feet.
Bitten.
Debauched.
Ruffled.
Devoid.
Baby spoon fed.
Oh, what a necessary slump indeed.

Teeming Streets

The streets teem full of plastic people
with plastic smiles and plastic souls
and soon enough they will have picked
all the wings off all the flies.
And no longer able to fly, those wingless flies
will fill those very same plastic streets
and hardship will fill the very air we all breathe.

Comfort will become such a rare commodity
that even the rich of the earth won't be able to afford it
except for a very few who will live in their plastic palaces.

As the human race races toward
another snowball earth phase
the talking heads shall speak of warming globes
and through it all I smile and laugh
but my smile isn't plastic just yet.
It's a smile, spare yet full,
at peace with moving fast
and wasting away.

Dry Stick and Baskets

The words seek a wider territory than I can provide.
Even my shadows are made thin-skinned
and temperamental.

I'm hanging on to this branch
like Hemingway held on to the shotgun
until the thing was done.

Night and day.
Day and night.

The boat is leaking dry sticks and baskets.

A Word That Begins with the Letter "L"

You could have taken anything but instead you took it all.
Where does a thing go when it's done?
What we had was as tolerable as anything can be,
all bound up in the sweet and wild flow
of leaping and wilted remains.

But the minor contentments
we filled each other with wasn't enough for you.
You wanted things dripping with mercy.
Reason.
Logic.
Even the "L" word.
To you that was the bare minimum.
A necessity.
Like air.
Like food.
Like water.

And now you are gone.
And now I'm alone again.
Dying from my refusal to exist in places
I'm afraid to be.

Black Coffee and Strawberries

Riding the elevator up, drinking black coffee
and eating strawberries,
aimlessly considering the pace of the tides.
Some people have never been to a madhouse.
Some spend a few weeks in a madhouse.
Some spend a lifetime.
Who knows what makes a delicious mind tick?
Regardless, the music in the elevator is there
but barely noticeable.

Like me sometimes.
Or you.

It sounds like an off key, hand-holding stepmother.
The guy next to me in the elevator
is slobbering all over himself
trying to eat pudding with a fork
and he smells like urine does after eating asparagus.

I am sure he has seen a madhouse.
Or will at some point in his life.
I'm certain of that.

I'm also certain
I will be taking the stairs down
on my return trip.

Not Yet

He had missed the boat.
Oh, he was standing on the dock and all.
But he found himself dreaming of the water
and being torn to shreds by the propeller blades.

He had missed the train.
Oh, he was standing on the station platform and all.
But he found himself frozen
by the thought of jumping onto the tracks
in front of a large freight.
Frozen by how real it felt.

He had missed the flight.
Oh, he was standing in the terminal and all.
But he found himself at some airport bar,
frozen by the thought of never seeing her again.

Guess he wasn't going anywhere after all.

Not yet anyway.

Below Average Lover

Some nights the wife is easy and consolable.
And some nights she offers
an 8-ounce Styrofoam cup kind of love.

No matter.
It's not like I'm going around trying to pull rabbits out of hats.
I'm just trying to get a quick dip in the dishwasher
before I go back to writing poorly and drinking swell swill.

Perhaps this is the confession of a below average lover
born of boredom and rusted gallows.
I fancy myself a trivial wall sconce of romance,
shone dimly and enclaved.

Why she stays I will never know.
But she does.
Or has so far anyway.

Overlooking a life wrought with rot.
She is my saber-toothed nest egg.
And I love her the only way I know how.

All of Us

The passers by of time and space.
The time passers taking up space.
Me, you, all of us.
We're the clogged drains.
We're the backed up dirty bath water
of a community shower.
We're the case of the unfortunate ones.
Me, you, all of us.
The alimony mongers.
The persistent tickles in the throat.
The whooping coughs with decadent discharge.

It could always be worse though,
that was my mantra for years.
It stopped working somewhere along the way,
I need a new mantra.

I drank right through all the wine of my youth.
Ran it bone dry.
Ran the cup from half full to half empty
to all the way empty,
then I smashed that god-damned thing
to splinters and shards.
And now I'm walking barefoot across the floor
where the shattered pieces landed,
and it cuts when I walk.

I'm bleeding all over this god forsaken place
and my cup now runneth over
with the blood of my sleepless nights
and tragic excuses for days
and I love every second out of which
my new-found hate is born.

Ode to the Simple Things

Wondering what ever happened from inside the madness.
Pure luck.
Pure gamble.
I might survive it.
I might not.
It all matters very little, if at all, and I know that.

I've been living on fumes for decades
and the motor's still churning.
So, to hell with the subject matters and improper contents.
If it needs to be written, then it will be written.
The problem is nothing truly needs to be written.

I write for me alone.
I drink for me alone.
I live for me alone.
And I'm going to die for me alone.

At best I will leave a bunch of half-assed poems behind
to be thrown in the dumpster with the rest.

It's where they belong.

Fixated

I love to look at her while she sketches.
Her eyes fixated on that sketch pad,
working that paper over and over and over.
Smudging the lead with her thumb.
Then pack to the pencil.
A fury of expression and passion and raw energy.

Then she works that eraser,
and eraser shavings start flying everywhere.
I love it!
So much creation that fills the air,
and I waft and I breathe in deep
so I can take it all in with her.
Share the experience with her.
And she allows it.

Once in a while I notice her noticing me
and it gives birth to a grin for both of us.
The type of grin that is glad that we were noticed
but shy at the same time.
Never any pretense, just art.

That she lets me watch
is one of my favorite things about her.
Sometimes she even lets me see the drawing
before it's done,
these are the special moments.

These are the moments that matter.

Densely Textured

Great lives, full of densely textured fire,
a delightful sort of crazy,
are rare in a time when words are so often wasted.
I figured I must be doing a decent job with this writing bit
because everybody seemed to hate what I wrote
when they read it.
No problem there.

I was told long ago, by a man much wiser than I,
that likeability in the language is certain death.
So, my pen stays in motion these days
and the next poem is all I'll ever seek.

This one here is for the hard working truly beatens.
It's for those who seldom go for the obvious.
For anyone feeling burned down again.
And most importantly it's for me.

Back Pocket Comfort

Woke up today feeling fully chewed to pieces
by the whole damn thing.
The sand in the motor.
The sugar in the gas tank.
The banana in the tail pipe of my existence.

All these wake ups, day after day.
All in an attempt not to die in my own excrement.

Time to look for the more relaxed lies.
Iron out the wave ripples in my Tibetan inspired rug.
I'm comforted by the flask I sleep with in my back pocket.
My sips like fire roasted purity.
My belly like flabby undercooked bacon.

I'm the bullet riddled sunflower amongst the flaxen maidens.
I'm the reason for the dirty ring in the bathtub.
But even late bloomers are useful sometimes, I'm told.
And I generally sneeze three sneezes at a time.
So, this morning al dente will have to do.

Nutshell

The soundless weeping of the fire gloom on the skids
is as real as anything else and I got some sharp as proof.
There is a recognition of the newness by the masses
when you are fresh meat but I'm old now
and my life goals consist of drinking and writing
and dying off soon enough.

When I'm gone they will be sure to check for accuracy
in the soft places I've been because they will want to know
who taught me how to apply the polish.

But I've had no teachers.
No gurus.
No familiar forms to speak of.

I'm just a man sickened to the root
who wasted far too much time
looking for clear eyes in a soft culture.

To Die a Noble Death

Well quaffed narcissism.
He used to have a lot of say back then.
Those early creative years.
But times change, things change, people change.
The real ones anyway.
The plastic ones stay humdrum,
irrelevant water cooler chatter.

He figured if he died a noble death
it would validate those early years and that early work.

Die like a mama's boy
defending the honor of the traditional sense.
Die drinking a bottle of red wine
in the late morning into early afternoon,
knowing it really hit the spot.
Die a dozen deaths, a dozen lipstick deaths.
Die the same death over and over.
Die saying the company line.
Die with the allure, romance and beauty
of a motion picture death.
Die eight hours at a time and never take your break.
You have a right to that break but don't take it
just because you know it's your right to have it.
And punch that clock at the end of each day
and die, die, die, die.

Laundry

He wasn't a proud man by any means.
But he did revel in the fact that he cleaned the lint trap
in the community dryer machines when most others didn't.
He wouldn't put it back in all the way either.
After his load was done, he would prop it up
crooked and cock-eyed
so when the next tenant came to use the machines
that lint trap would be on display
for the world to see that it shone clean.

It was $3.50 a load, that's wash and dry,
as long as you didn't choose one of the fancy settings.
Highway robbery robbed of its integrity.

But it's a small price to pay for laundering your dirty bits
in pajamas and slippers and bathing caps
and unshaven faces and unshaven legs.

He found his peace in those lint traps.
He found the washing away of his past there too.

Faces

So many faces; so many, many faces.
People want everything to be cute.
Mickey Mouse.
But it's not all cute; far from it.

I love my ugly.
My swollen potbelly.
My hang-ups and let downs.
My bad breath after buffalo chicken and coffee.
My arm pitted, sweat stained work shirts.
My corny jokes.
My clearing my throat and spitting,
twice, three times and again.
My fingernail and finger skin biting
and fingernail and finger skin bit pieces on the floor.
My butt scratching.
My finger smelling.
My stinky belly button lint trap.
My nostril hairs.
My drunk stumbling.
My food stuck in my teeth.
My open mouth chewing.
My smelly bowel movements.
My sweaty back and ass on hot days.
My inner ear picking.
My flicking of my ear wax.
My belching and blowing it in your face.
My rotten gut gas stench.
My obsessive thoughts.
My beautiful filth.
My beautiful disgust.
My beautiful me.

Eight Stories Up

The window is eight stories up
and it looks like a fine flight down.
Reckless flights of fancy.
It's not so easy to do.
One foot out, one foot in.
Make your choice, can't have it both ways.
Leaps of faith and cracked windshields
and spider webs wound too tight.
With shooting stars ablaze
how could she be so mean to me?

The window is eight stories up
and it looks like a fine flight down.
Waiting, wanting and yearning.
Longing, needing and pining.
Two feet out, leaning forward,
fingers gripped to window moldings.
Too sentimental for our own good
we cling and climb and grope
in those dark, dank places of dwelling and dealing.

The window is eight stories up
and it looks as if she has arrived after all.
Looks like the flight has been cancelled.

No Legs

Its 7:13 on a Tuesday morning and I'm sitting at a red light
that seems to shine brighter than red lights usually do.
I look to the right.
On the sidewalk a legless man in a motorized wheelchair
pulls up and stops at that same bright-ass red light.
He's got style.
I can tell.
He's decorated his wheelchair with anti-establishment stickers,
a flag and what looks like side saddlebags.
He's ready for the fight.
He motions for me to roll down my window.
I oblige.

"Wanna race jackass?" he snarls.
I tell him I do.
I roll up the window and stare back at the light.
Then back at no legs.
Then the light again.
It turns green.
I punch it.
I'm out of the gate quick.
He can't match what's under my hood.

I quickly see him fading in the distance of my rear view
with a big smile and his middle finger
flying as high as his "don't tread on me" flag
that's blowing in the wind.

I drive on to work knowing full well
this is the only race I'm winning today.

Come a Long Way

Almost done in, but not quite.
I'm still here, you see?
We've come a long way since Leviticus, you know?
But a mighty long way still to go, you dig?
On the outside looking in at your junior proms.
On the outside looking in at your senior citizens.
On the inside looking out at your sneers, jeers and fears.
Hard to catch your breath with a boot on your throat.
Hard to catch the boot with your hands tied behind your back.

We all need a reason to wake up, you see?
We all got invited on the journey, you know?
We all get used and pushed around, you dig?
Hard to speak with your tongue cut out.
Hard to stop the blade with your hands cut to shreds.
Hard to believe, I know, but I'm still here.

Broken Heart Smiles

"What can I get for you sir?" The waitress asked
with the zeal of someone still believing in life.

He suddenly noticed her mouth was shaped like a heart
not yet broken and he reminisced for a moment.

"I'll have a tequila. A double please.
No need for training wheels with it."

"I'm sorry, but I'm not sure what training wheels
with tequila are, sir."

"It just means I don't need the salt or the lime sweetie."

"Oh, ok." She said with a smile and a laugh
that caused that heart to break.

*Funny how easily a woman's smile and laugh
can break a heart like that
... just like that.* he thought..

King of the Slackers

Sitting here on a serene Saturday
sipping on the sanity sauce,
not pressing the thing,
just passing time in the leisurely ways.
The kids are running around playing.
The grill is warming up.
Life makes sense in this moment.
So I'm breathing with a bit more awareness
than usual today.

I want to notice it.
I want to notice it all.
I know it won't last.
Can't last.
I wouldn't want it to.
I can only stomach so many happy time poems.

But this is one.
And it's not even hastily written,
but writing with haste is usually the point.
Living with haste is usually the point.
But not today.

Today the machine is in a low gear.
Notebook in hand.
Pen in hand.
And a slow burning fire between the ears.

Rear View Mirror

The moans and hollers echo from the forever war
that is, was and ever will be.
The bravado is lost.
The thrill is gone.

Oh, to B.B. King for a day would have been so fine.
But I too have known a few Lucilles in my time.
And they all said the same thing.

It's all about balance.
It's all about groove.
Sound moods and reflections be damned.

Rusty Nail

Nearing high noon
with the sun blazing its churn,

I sit under a tree filled with birds,
grateful I haven't been shit on yet.
At least not by the birds.

The dense brutality of the waking world
is a different matter altogether.
I feel like combing these poems out of my teeth
with the rigor of a horny ape;
it's all that's keeping me out of the nut house.

A tightening grip of hot tongs
is unrelenting on my balls as I think about it.
Time to raise the coward's flag and fly it high.

The carpets on fire
seem too broad for leaping these days.

It's all smothered biscuit gravy maneuverings
and faucet drips.

I just pray the nail isn't rusty
when I step on it.

Stories Written

Wading the gentle pools of obscurity and failure.
Leaping the bluffs in a stupor.

At last.
At last.

Twilight lay beneath the veil at last.
Longing.
Longing.
Lonely at heart.

Wake me when art is allowed to be art.

All the Same

Their minds are starved.
No food for thought to be found.

Mindless channel surfing.
Water cooler sports chatter.

Strolling to our graves, hands in our pockets,
whistling a happy tune, we fill our time just fine.

Bowling alleys and bar room brawls,
it's all the same.

Philosophical chat rooms and billiard halls,
it's all the same.

College classrooms and street corners,
it's all the same.

Father Time speaks unconditional truths.
Even the young ones get old eventually.

Bound to Lesser Things

Breathing heavy.
Chest is pumping.
And all I did is climb a flight of stairs.

My mind is a clotted mass of decaying drivel this morning.
Well worth its price of admission though.

I was caught in the most wonderful, soft silken wanderlust
of kimchi and rice wine last night.
Went to an engagement party for friends
at a dive Korean joint.

My wife says she spent the night
trying to school me in the proper chopstick technique
but instead I insisted on stabbing at the different foods
with one of my sticks.

I don't remember but I believe her.
I was more interested in the sake anyhow.

Car Doors

A woman loves to have her car door opened for her.
She is willing to overlook so many shortcomings
once you open that door.

She'll forget all about a man's lack of sophistication.
She'll forget all about the times you came home late.
The times you came home drunk,
too drunk to perform on those nights
she was dying to feel you inside her.
The times you didn't notice her new hair style
or weight loss or new outfit.
The times you pretended to be listening.

All is forgiven once you open that passenger door
and gently caress her back as she slides into that seat.
She allows you to make her feel the elegance
that she keeps tucked away in those distant, private places.
And she deserves it.

Women have been putting up with us for a long time.
And they will continue to look the other way
as long as we keep opening those car doors.

Tilted

I had met him when he was on the brink of his fame.
Within minutes of making his acquaintance I could tell
that everything I had heard about him was likely true.
From what I had been told and understood,
he was equal parts insane and genius.
A wonderful combination to be sure.

He was the type that saw hangovers
as a small price to pay for a short-lived peace of mind
and I understood that all too well.
I noticed his head seemed to tilt to the right when he spoke.
I watched him from a corner at the opposite end of the room
and sure enough, every time he opened his mouth to speak
his head would tilt a noticeable right-handed tilt.
And when he was done talking, sure enough,
it would straighten right back up.
I found myself standing, drink in one hand,
scratching my head with the other, wondering
if my head would tilt like that one day too.

Flush

Glorious is the view from the top turnbuckle.
To hell with remorse.
Guilt.
Apologies.
Time to start running toward the men holding the shovels.
I'll ask only one last favor.
Cover me good, boys, don't miss an inch.
And let the worms get to work.
Stripping the meat down to the bone
so I can be beautiful for once.
The curtain has drawn on the self-pity bit.
Seems silly, now, to have spent so much time juicing carrots.
And kale.
And ginger.

The bad years still shone through a face
gut wrenched and slathered.
Red eyed and wet brained.

A man whose poems worked well as toilet paper.
A privilege to wipe the asses of accidental readers.

Flush.
Flush.
Flush.

Clearly Dissipated

I'm sitting here trying to remember
but also trying to forget.
I'm failing on both counts.

It's one of those moments
when the music doesn't even sound good.
That's when you know it's a rough go.
I think of her face often, as I am now.

She had a face that seemed to mean everything
and nothing all at once.
A face that made my life difficult
but I know it would have been far worse without it.

She made the nothing times worthwhile
while being my reason for getting through the days
and through the nights.

The nature of human nature is beguiling indeed.

I'm a man with.
I'm a man without.
I'm a man clearly dissipated.

Dichotomy Yes

Yes to corn bread and three-day weekends.
Yes to free food and free liquor.
Yes to long walks off short piers.
Yes to moments of self-doubt.
Yes to moments of confidence.
Yes to moments of fear
        giving rise to moments of clarity.
Yes to sunny days.
Yes to winter nights
        with hot chocolate and movie marathons.
Yes to buffets
        and cheap wine gulped out of Styrofoam cups.
Yes to friends in need.
Yes to friends with weed.
Yes to sugary cereal with soy milk.
Yes to candlelight dinners on paper plates.
Yes to viewing life from the periphery.
Yes to anonymous random acts of kindness.
Yes to love.
Yes to laughing.
Yes to crying.
Yes to self-help.
Yes to being beyond help.
Yes to planning for the future.
Yes to living for today.
Yes to binge drinking.
Yes to early morning runs (both kinds).
Yes to dry skin and moisturizing lotion often.
Yes to neuroticism.
Yes to vulnerability.
Yes to processed foods and vitamins.
Yes to using words
        that may or may not in fact fit the context.
Yes to back scratchers
        with extending arms.

Yes to hiking
        in the woods.
Yes to walking
        along city streets.
Yes to beer bellies.
Yes to travel.
Yes to hermit lifestyles.
Yes to both sides of the fence.
Yes to deep breaths.
Yes to computer match making.
Yes to love making
        at all times of day, in all areas of a home.
Yes to faith.
Yes to doubt.
Yes to organized chaos.
Yes to haircuts and comb-overs.
Yes to loving to live
        while living to die.
Yes to hard work.
Yes to proud slacking.
Yes to book smarts.
Yes to street smarts.
Yes to dieting
        coupled with gluttony.
Yes to vegetarian appetizers
        and red meat entrees.
Yes to foot rubs.
Yes to back and front rubs.
Yes to drunken afternoon sex.
Yes to nightfall sober love making.
Yes to yin
        and yes to yang.
Yes to black, white and grey.
Yes to tall pint glasses.
Yes to short shot glasses.
Yes to lending a helping hand.
Yes to accepting a helping hand.

May all the days and nights of your lives
        be lived from a place of yes!

Sawdust

Crows don't sleep with peacocks
while lonely hearts wail.

Sometimes the sawdust spills out a little
on the floor and mixes with the gloom
and stains the impotent pieces of paper strewn about.

Better off simply walking into the sun.
But it's too cold for that.
So just walk on the sun.

What a glorious non lyrical,
non-singing thing that would be.

Gets to Drinking

Bumbling around the futility.
Looking sad in the sun
having been fattened up by experience.
The scoundrel gets to drinking heavy
and thick with compulsion.
Getting whipped by the rapid rotations.
Made to feel at ease.

The louse gets to drinking while ceilings and walls
watch us settle old scores.
Playing dirty rotten tricks in a dirty rotten world.
On a battlefield of a war not meant to be won.

The wretch gets to drinking gallons
of all things useless, vain and dull.
I suppose he drinks because he knows all the answers.
But he just can't or won't tell us.
Not sure which or either.
It matters not.

Now let's all get to drinking
shall we?

Crumbling

Nerves made raw peering out at sunny days
while another school building is shot to bits and pieces.

So many guns.
So many, many guns.
The Q-tip has clearly dug too deep.

It is too late.
It is far too late.
The empire is crumbling before us.

Mighty and Dry

I've always felt an overwhelming gravitational pull
to the word.
And the pen.
And the notebooks.
And the way they all dance so effortlessly together.
Weaving bits of meaning
and exploring the meaning of things.

But some days the words just don't want to arrive.
They stay tucked away in corners.
Keeping a low profile, stubborn and haunting.

Today my mind is screaming
the yelp of the fire dancers
as I try to squeeze out as much juice as possible.

But I'm dry.
I'm dry.
Like a mouthful of sand.

I'm mighty and dry.

Strange Companions

Phantoms furious and elusive.
What does love look like?
Taste like?
Smell like?
Feel like?
To some unknown.
To some never known.
I cry for those without, those who never see it.
Never taste it.
Never smell it.
Never feel it.

They didn't seem to make much sense as a couple.
But then again life didn't seem to make much sense either
so I suppose you could consider it a wash.

She was a good foot taller than him.
And a good foot wider too.
And they were in love. Real, true love.
Not the vending machine, turn of a knob for a quarter
and see what pops out kind of love. This was REAL.

And for some reason people seemed to go out of their way
to point out the odd nature of their look together.
And they didn't care.
And I told them often that I felt they made a lovely couple.
And every time we were all together we drank and laughed.
And snorted when we laughed.
And laughed until our tears came.
And went on and on and on and on
and we would always close-down whatever joint we were in.
We allowed ourselves to be ourselves,
even if only for these moments.
I hold on tight to the hope
that I might have a love like theirs one day too.

Sans

The beer gut gets strangled by the belt
and fingertips get chewed to the nub
while children are force fed fairy tales
with pumpkin pie farces
and white picket fences served a la mode.

A great day for staring at light bulbs, I say.
Or walking nameless blank streets
in search of accidental gargoyles
perched immobile in death's anticipation.

Oh my!
A walk sans destination.
Soul searching sans soul.
A vigorous chewing sans food.

Meanwhile all the king's horses
shit on all the king's men.

I hold out zero hope
of ever being put back together again.

Nonetheless

The sky was yellow that day
and almost seemed wine soaked
but the raindrops fell dry.
And that night there was no moon at all.

It was then that I realized there is beauty in the dirt.
In the sickness.
In the violence.
In the hopelessness.

It's a beauty loud and indifferent.
But a beauty, nonetheless.

Free Verses

Dealing now with the unpleasant aspects of the thing.
The real and immediate terrain not yet explored.
I am a rancid bitterness thrusting against restraint
with no wasted motions in these words.

8 years' worth.
10 years' worth.
A lifetime worth of free verses and farewells
on behalf of the working class and sifting streams.

There is a hurt relentless and a pain unforgiving
that the majority are forced to endure
each day and each night,
the same as it's always been.

Fleeting relief lies in the barkeeps hand.
We reach for the grinning surges.
With this in mind I raise my glass
but today I find no relief to speak of.

Watching the Lemmings

To the darling billions of you
who chose to get out of bed this morning
(oh yes, my friend, it was most certainly a choice) I salute you.
Day after day, year after year,
we crawl out of our protective caves at a snail's pace,
in a rat race, heading bravely into the fire,
fascinating in our commitment to carry on the charade.

       Alarm clock.
       Bathroom.
       Coffee maker.
       Food shoveled down.
       Shower.
       Start car.
       Drive.

It's with a profound sense of pleasure
that I am choosing to stay in my bed
on this crisp winter morning,
proudly deferring to my inner sloth.
I wish I could tell you of a guilt-ridden moment
as I call the big boss and explain
he will not have the pleasure of my company
on this fine day, but that would be a lie.
I am officially 24 hours free of the machine.
I plan to eat eggs smothered in cheese and hot sauce
while standing at the window watching the lemmings drive off
toward their employment cliffs and retirement ledges.

And tomorrow I will have to re-join the herd, rest assured,
but today I feel damn good.
It's with my bathrobe wide open and bare assed
that I salute you all once again,
and I truly hope you enjoy your ride in.

Spit Out

I don't know how the bee got in the can.
Or maybe it was a wasp.
But it didn't really matter
because it was no longer in the can.

It was now in my mouth and stinging the hell out of me.
I could feel each bitter insert
as if deliberate in its placement
and it must have been 5 or 6 strikes
before I realized that opening my mouth
would most certainly improve my life circumstance.

I spit out the mouthful and sure enough
I saw the culprit riding its liquid exit.
My first thought was to end its life,
a swift death sentence issued by the victim of the crime.

Actually, that was my second thought.
My first thought was god dammit my mouth hurts.
But regardless, a trial was not coming the perpetrators way.
It was straight to the executioner's block for this little fucker.

And then something swept over me.
A wave of empathy.
Every time life has swallowed me up
I've fought like hell to break free too.
We were kindred spirits.
Me and this little fighter.

I watched him dart away
and I went back to drinking my can.

Dwindling Moonlight

The moonlight is dwindling as emperors weep
and the birds are fast asleep.
The years are mellowing my madness
but that's alright,
there are still plenty of pints left to be had.

And there will always be final storms raging,
ever oblique, for the dead who still can't speak.

Time

Minds sit waiting in the belly of the overblown,
often asking where the time has gone.

Once young, undisturbed
and full of unexplained whimsy
the sage has now turned to stone,
yet still throws some light into the dark.

We must bore through the senses
and the illusions in revelatory anticipation
toward the invisible realms,
for a man may be born on one day
and die on another
but what happens between the hyphen
is in fact where the time has gone.

Belt Buckle

Dropping a quarter, 2 dimes and a nickel
into a piggy bank for beer money
is like trying to stick a fork into a rock
or taking a gulp from the dive bar community spittoon.

A genius of a flattened age scratches his belly.
Checks the belly button for lint.
Smells the finger for good measure.
And admires the Texas sized belt buckle
he received in the mail yesterday
from a distant admirer of his work.

He seems satisfied.
The kiss of death.
He's done.

Release the Grip

Trimming my beard and mustache at two in the morning
makes sense to me.
Women don't.
When it comes to my women problems
I'm quite aware that I am in fact the problem.
I'm certain of this.

I'm becoming an old dog
trying to hang on for dear life to my inner pup,
but I have no real interest in learning any new tricks.

An inspiration long dwindling,
telling me to "just let go old boy".
Release the grip.
The temptress lies in wait around every corner,
biding her time.

I invite her in.
I offer her a drink.
I make her feel sexy.
I put the dagger in her hand.
I raise her arm.
Then I walk slowly towards her
without as much as a whimper.

A Delving Day

Look how they get so soft.
Well-manicured by the conveniences of way too easy.
Maybe they would be better served to hit a bad patch.
A rough stretch.

Maybe they need to learn to hate themselves a little deeper.
Maybe they need to feel
the "two in the morning can't sleep",
and know they deserve it skid.

Maybe they need
the "treat your woman poorly yet again, only to regret it"
and know she didn't deserve it skid.
A little self-loathing goes a long way my friends.

Maybe they would be better served
to embrace the lunacy of a mind long broken.
Digest the cycles.
Eat them for breakfast.
Digest the hopelessness.
Feast on it for lunch.
Devour the doubt.
Glutton upon it at supper time.
Chew it all up real good and proper.

Now. swallow it down with no water to help.
And pray you choke.
Heave, gag, gasp and cough.
Then find a notebook and write a poem.

Be Sure

Be sure to take off your shoes before walking into the fire.
Be sure to run with scissors, blade out, wildly through life.
Be sure to give away every last possession you own
before you die.

Be sure to stare directly into the sun.
Be sure to feed your vegetables to the dog under the table.
Be sure to jump into the swimming pool as soon
as a big meal is finished
and be sure you ate your dessert first.

Be sure to look only one way before crossing the street.
Be sure to partake in fun and games knowing full well
someone may get an eye poked out.
Be sure to leap without looking.
Be sure to spend your money as soon as you get it
to ensure it does not, in fact, burn a hole in your pocket.
Be sure to burn bridges down to ashes and smoldering cinders.
Be sure to ride your bike with no helmet
and no reflectors and on the wrong side of the street.
Be sure to dance in the rain in a lightning storm,
holding an umbrella with a metal tip.

Be sure to do everything
you were ever taught or told NOT to do
and maybe, just maybe, you will survive.

Bottle the Moments

What to do while waiting for answers
with a mind that's been black market approved?

Whatever I choose to do I will do it for Hamp.
Do it for Red.
Do it for Bags.
Do it for Cal.
Do it for Monk.
Do it for Trane.
Do it for Mulls.
Do it for Lockjaw.

I will hold on for dear life
to something that isn't there
as I bottle the moments.
Bottle the bile.
Bottle the easy struttin' blues walk.
Uncork the bottle and take a slug.
I'll stay slugging it hard
as the guillotine drops and crowd applauds.

With a Capital H

It's all moving further away.
The past and the future.

What's the definition of love?

Love is the morning fog before the sun comes up.
Love is that little while until the fog burns away.
Quick and absolute, burning away toward the first day light.
Carrying itself like a big galoot.
Love has a heavy face with heavy features.
Love is being at odds with the rest.
But for how long you may ask?

Too long.

Love is a childhood horror story.
That's horror with a capital H.
Good times never come without a price.
Good times never come free; you see?

Apartment Thiefdom

Immortalized yet again.
Like a wet dog caught out in the rain.
Kudos to the inventor of the sandwich.
I'll take a ham with mustard and toss half to the seagulls.
Wash the other half down with straight bourbon.
Wash it down with undiluted hatred.

Time to listen to my fists while making a call on a payphone.
Shadowbox with my belief systems.
Press pause and let the sirens scream bye.
Press play to resume and toss poems to those same seagulls
while the opera singer serenades.

Walk into the wrong apartment in the wrong complex
on the wrong day and drink their wine.
Drink their scotch.
Drink their beer.
But be sure not to kill their cockroaches.
That way they will never even know you were there.

Chipped Tooth Gnaw

Buzzed in the dawning a.m. hours yet again
and I realize I just may live forever after all.
Tipsy as the mid-morning wanes yet again
and I realize I just may be able to fly after all.
Drunk at noon yet again
and I realize how cliché my life truly is.

Forty years old and yet to cast a ballot,
never voted even once.
Mayors, Governors and Presidents are elected
as I gnaw at a twenty-dollar bill through chipped teeth.
Chalk it up to a life of losing
before the starting gun was even fired.

What is the force that holds any of us up?
Luck?
Maybe.
Circumstance?
Probably.
Birth rights?
Apparently.

Don't get me wrong,
the underdog manages a victory once in a while.
But don't worry,
the earth still goes on spinning just fine when they do.

Leaps of Faith

Like some screaming thing.
Weeping for mercy or something similar.
With no place to go and nothing you can do.

The balcony no longer seems that high up.
But you haven't grown wings.
And you haven't learned to fly.
And suicide is still a permanent haste.

So read the letter again
and make sure the words are still there.
And if the words are still there
make sure they haven't changed.
And remember there are unopened beer bottles
in the fridge needing tending to.

So leaps of faith will have to wait.
At least for now.

And you have a dentist appointment tomorrow.
So it may have to wait a couple of days.
Because who wants to die with a toothache.

Life Observations

Throw the ears of corn across the room.
Burn the franks in the pan on the stove top.
In you I see great potential for larger things.
I see it written on the cardboard drink coasters
sitting in front of you.
I never meant to put lime juice in your salt, I swear it.
Forgiveness is offered with an eerie calm, golden in hue.
There appears to be ghosts around every corner,
 must be time for a fresh start.

This town is growing smaller with each day.
Dare not stay to close to home
but dare not to venture too far either;
life may lose its sentimental value.

Be wise to be careful,
impunity is a rare commodity.

These are just a few life observations.
And I am sharing them with you.

Tightened Belts

Test the cliff's edge.
Start a fire just to blow it out.
But don't poke the bear with a cigarette.
Beer guts get pinched in tightened belts
like deflated high hopes and gale force wind sea-swells.

Skip the oil changes to seize up the engine.
Put a slow leak in the rear passenger tire and wait.
Just wait.
And wait some more.
Soon enough we all go flat.

If Only

At the local public library.
Sitting.
Writing.
Watching.

The snow is falling gracefully outside
and I can see it through the window
on the far end of the aisle.

Just a moment of peace.
That's all this is.

I will accept it as such.
As it is.

If only we could do this for each other,
ask of each other to be only what we are.
Never more than that.

Oh, what a meadow lark that would be indeed!

Snowed In

Snowed in and glad about it.
Able to finally relax,
albeit only for a precious few days.

Snowed in and glad about it.
Three days snowed in.
Three days unshowered.
Three days unshaven.
Three days uncombed.
Three days disheveled.
Three days delirious.

Two feet of snow.
Two feet unshoveled.
Two feet unplowed.
Two feet untouched.

Looking upon the horizon
and still no sign of spring.
And I'm glad about it.

Adjusting Creatures

I have no idea about reverberating notes of a harpsichord.
But I do know there is a way of loving smog.
Just take a long breath and become part of it.
We are all just creatures adjusting to conditions.

Like the men with perfectly quaffed mustaches
sitting around drinking wine and talking about themselves.
Listening to that is when my nerves finally reach the throat.
My hands stuffed into empty pockets as all the rivers run dry.

Just remember, starving doesn't create art.
It creates hunger pangs.
Now chew on that.

Curious Buzzings

The most beautiful factors, relentless,
carry a heavy sleep
if just given a chance.

Old guys like me,
so easily pleased by short stays of luck
and nights of overture,
are seeking deeper ways
in our otherwise meaningless existences.

A delightful scratch here
or a curling of gentle words there
to put a new frame around the thing.
Giant steps indeed.

And tonight a hurricane in female form
sits next to me
riding a high swelled wave of babble
and a never waning edge of molten bursts.
And I love her fire.
And I love her gathered hums.

She offers this old man curious buzzings
in places peaceable and well hidden.

Music-less Sockets

It can finally be deadening.
Day after day.
Having to gaze into their music-less sockets for eyes.

Endless peering into the long silence
of a drowning nothing.
Quite a luxury.
To be simple and uninvolved.

At my favorite bar
I would always use the same bathroom stall intentionally
just to read what some pooping prophet
had scrawled for the world to read:
"Just go with it, it's all meaningless anyway"

I couldn't agree more.

Eventually

Have you any idea?
Have you any idea how many beatings that is?
Hung up on after the first sentence.
Beatings offer lessons.
Life teachings.

And writing inspirations.
But where's the link?
The link is your back against the wall.
The link is your breaking point.
The link is a tendency to say what you mean.
The link is honesty.

In other words, all the pretense
will eventually be beaten out of you.
The meaning of pain as a literary teacher.
Pain without reason?
Well give that pain some reason then.

Left to our own devices
we often waste the painful blessings.
You would be surprised.
You would be surprised
how much blood is in a person.
It's a rough trip but we all must eventually let go.

Rise in the Glass

Side stepping the mountains
in order to arrive at death.
Only to find more time.

Watching the walls is a harmless habit.
But rarely does anything happen.

Better to open the beer.
Pour the beer.
Watch it rise in the glass.
Smell the beer.
Drink the beer with fury.

Then the answers will surely come
spinning into sight as you take a big bite
into the unripe parts of life
and continue to pick at the cuticle beds
of nonexistence.

My Share

I've come to understand
that manure is a part of the fragrance of the roses
and it's taken a few rounds of eternity to know this,
but it has come right when it seems I'm hitting my stride.

Saying this is a precursor to the obvious:
When two crazy hearts are pumping in synch
all else is shoved aside.

So let's enjoy our last little swims
with an asphyxiated twinkle in our eyes
because trouble never stops arriving,
it merely changes its course sometimes.

And I know I'm overdue for my share.

Bad News First

Navigation in life is seeking the walkable bridges,
stepping back from the pompous and resisting the complex.
Some writers live in the woods to find it.
Some writers need spiral staircases and train tracks to feel it.

I get it from places rancid and soft.
My simple lines are meant to run
with the ease of one last time.

I knew a blues singer once
who drove unblinkingly through roads too narrow
and always asked the doctors
to hit him with the bad news first.
And he asked them to give it to him slowly.

Last Drink of the Night

She is like a sunset within a heart,
        more pure than the last drink of the night.
She is like the silence of far off bravery,
        more pure than the last drink of the night.
She is like the admission of jealousy,
        more pure than the last drink of the night.
She is like the soft sound of snow pelting the porch screen
during the first snowfall of winter's season,
        more pure than the last drink of the night.
She is like the loosening of a white knuckled grip,
        more pure than the last drink of the night.
She is like the moment a writer finds their voice
after being blocked and pent up,
        more pure than the last drink of the night.
She is like the color yellow itself,
        more pure than the last drink of the night.
She is like the first sips of a cold drink on a hot day,
        more pure than the last drink of the night.
She is like a prize fighter's resolve
to answer the bell of the final round,
        more pure than the last drink of the night.
She is like the twenty-dollar bill
found unexpectedly in a pant pocket,
        more pure than the last drink of the night.

She is all these things to me and so much more.

Yet to Move

He we all are.
Rare it would be seen.
Squinty eyed.
Forlorn.
Ok.
Ok.

But how could you not like nature?
Oh, nature is just fine.
Too damn repetitive though.
The trees.
The countryside.
Hills.
Valleys.
Bored and lulled.

The earth's time moves too slowly
for human appreciation.
Easier to nod off.
Or stick a finger up in defiance.
The middle one?
Too cliché.
A pinky perhaps?
Too small to get the job done.
Just point then.
Point and shoot.

Down goes Frazier.
And the mountains have yet to move.

Dumb Luck

A hilarious confusion.

It'll be alright.
It'll be alright.
It'll be alright.

Out of the way destination points,
let's toast to a life lived off the beaten path.
Wherever do you get your concepts from, man?
Love brings its own agonies with it,
endurance is more important than valuable anyhow.
I feel rather foolish, nothing but dumb luck.
But that counts for something too,
just promise you won't let it consume you.
Lying on the floor gutted,
sometimes a man falls on his own knife.
In a general state of disrepair,
looking forward to the twilight,
we do those things anyway.
Sometimes there's just nothing left to hold onto,
closets are emptied
and clothes are thrown out onto front lawns.

It'll be alright.
It'll be alright.
It'll be alright.

Pay No Mind

Ceaseless obedience to the heart,
lighting tomorrow with today.
The winds of grace will always remain
blowing above vast sea spaces.
Neither stars nor ocean can hold a man.
Now advance with confidence.

Lavishly lap in the luxury of the ordinary
and work out your own salvation.
Pay no mind to the femme fatale's
sweet tasting sour digestion.

Two kinds of light shine with a beautiful clarity,
one illuminates while one obscures.
Be true to one's word.
Be true to one's work.
For just stepping out the door
can be a dangerous business.

Allow yourself to be swept away,
it's not enough to simply be industrious.

Sun, sand and hammocks.
Allow your toes to be tickled by the ocean
for that is virtue.

The middle ground is home to the masses.
Make your home a higher ground.
Return love for their hate.
Include those whom they have excluded.
And admit when you're wrong.
Never end your pursuit.
Continue to chase the wild things.

For A Time

For a time it was tequila.
Mostly tequila.
Some beer.
Some wine.
But mainly tequila.
One shot nip bottles.
Half pint bottles.
Full pint bottles.
Plastic handle jug bottles.
In my cargo pant pockets.
In my carry bag.
In my car glove box.
All over the house.
I just loved tequila.
Led to some of the best days and nights
I will never remember.

But nowadays I don't drink much tequila.
Sometimes I miss it.
Most times I don't.
But I'm thankful for the chapter.
Lots of stories in that chapter.
If only I could remember some.

A Little Is Plenty

What is needed?
A little silence.
A little love.
A little humanity.
Ingredients of a fragrant existence.

Never undertake your blessings without courage,
remember you are not alone.
Also remember that your home is within you,
be sure to furnish it wisely and with care.
The danger lies more in those things we desire
than those things we fear.
Simplicity embraced yet again.

Ancient Beginnings

Masters of antiquity
prove true to the mind that is still.
       Depths of wonder.
       Subtle mysteries discerned.
          Hesitant.
          Cautious.
          Solemn.
          Opaque.

Not overfilled
but gradually we come to life.
       Resist.
       Persist.
       Desist.
       Insist.
          Preserve and create anew.

If an image is imageless
we call it enigmatic.
       Confront it.
       Follow it.
       Encompass it.
          It can't be seen.

Wisdom of the ancients
proves true to the mind that is still.
       Not bright.
       Neither dark.

All forms and formless
return to nothingness eventually.

Back to our ancient beginnings.

Vivid Reminders

Thick paint brush strokes
on a taut canvas are vivid reminders.
Yet still, butterflies return to the same trees a year later.

Jagged sea glass edges
worn smooth to the touch are vivid reminders.
Yet still, the spring air is filled with birdsong a year later.

Viewpoints of love perched on high.
To see her face again is all a man ever wants.

The journey of a love affair ablaze.
To see her face again is all this man ever needed.

Merely Wanes

Garble the voices just to throw nails.
Like passing through a thing.
Again, again and again.
Creation being the true factor.
Death doesn't seem too bad after all.
Finally I'll be let out of the straight jacket.
Going mad is fine as long as it's a clean version.
It's the sloppy tides I can't stand to bear.

Maybe it's the novelty bird feeders.
Maybe it's the velvet lined dreams.
Maybe it's circling answer D on a multiple-choice exam.

The end is the beginning.
The beginning is the end.
The middle merely wanes.

All Inclusive

Woken up to a vacant snore
reminiscent of all-inclusive cruises and softball leagues.
It's time to cure the obvious so the subtle can infect.

With the power still out from the storm the night before,
I'm sure the beer is warm by now.
But warm beer beats no beer
and temperature is rather a state of mind anyhow.
Like having your soul biopsied
and being afraid of the results.
Like the air thick with people
playing word games.

Open a beer.
Take a slug.
A big slug.
Take another.
To be off kilter in the most pleasant of ways.
Now finish the beer.
Grab another.

Take a deep breath in
and prepare for the day to wilt.

Romantic Suicide

I lied to her and told her the tattoos didn't hurt too bad
when I got them.
She didn't believe me but said she did.
I liked when she did that.
She had the resilience of a child left behind.
And I liked that about her too.
She had a face cranberry red floating in wine.

To say I miss her would be an understatement.
No words could suffice.
Her way was the easiest I've ever known.
And her eyes the brightest that ever shone.

Hers made for a very romantic suicide.

Dampened

With the patience of an angler
dangling silken strands I wait.
And the tears won't come.

Through ice ages I wait.
As the continents drift, I wait.
Through volcanic rebirths I wait.
And the tears still won't come.

The broad stroke horizons
fog a dampened understanding.

Maybe that's why I can't cry so loud.

Ma Dukes

An older woman we met at the bar
who calls herself Ma Dukes
invited us to her house
so she could play her bongo drums for us
and show us her artwork she claimed she made
by painting her pussy hair
and laying down on large canvases.

When we arrived at her house
we realized she had 2 bongo drums
and many, many paintings.

She asked if
we would like to see her painting process live.
We said no thanks.
She asked if we would like to buy a painting.
We said no thanks.

She asked if we wanted a beer.
We said very much so.
Then she played the drums for us.

To this day she has yet to sell a painting.

Alimony Coals

Swollen with listlessness
I rise to answer a phone that rings but is out of key.
It's a man's voice on the other end.
An unfamiliar voice.
The man sounds as if he is wearing suspenders and a bowtie.
He says he is a divorce attorney and is representing
my in the process of becoming ex-wife.
I congratulate him.
He laughs an uncomfortable laugh.
Then there's silence.

In that moment I realize
I shall soon be raked over the alimony coals,
to be burnt and bloodied and bankrupt into submission
by the non-existent line between love and hate.

Women always say it's not about the money.
They say it's about a principle of sorts.
But it's always about the money.

Greedy throngs of bitter faced slotherly
banging down court-house doors.
They figure the not so good sex
they gave you not very often
is worthy of a hefty repayment plan.
And their lawyers figure it's so.
And the judges figure it's so.
So it must be so.

Nothing

When you are something,
something will always be expected of or from you.
When you are nothing,
nothing is ever expected of or from you.

The older I get the more I strive for nothing.
An ever more splendid nothing that can seem obtuse.
But still it's my lighthouse.
Nothing can be so beautiful.
Nothing can be so perfect.
Spinning on its crooked axis.
But it's also freeing.
Liked cracked mirror reflections.
Or screaming as you drown.

People never want reasonable answers
to reasonable questions
so I move away with my sundry bits,
somewhere between the art and the fire,
and accept that only rarely
will the Tupperware lids match their bottoms.

Human Nature

To be crazy.
To know it.
To not care.
That is the soiled genius.

There have been plenty nights spent alone
staring into the mirror at the white hairs
peeking through, my youth long since slinking away.
Becoming the rusted out old Ford in the picture
surrounded by lobster buoys.
The yellow paint still noticeable but fading
deeper to faintly with each season worn,
drowning in its own juices.

But tonight I'm made young again
as I go off to meet the little lady of my shining hour.
I walk out the door.
Reach the machine.
Throw two bottles in the right-side saddle bag
and start out in the direction opposite the sunset,
mocking the weakness of human nature.

Contemplate

Most people miss the point
of the thousand-year-old root system.

The tree gets it.
The one eared painter gets it.
The child speaking her first word gets it.
The monk in the cave sworn to silence gets it.

Through lingering scents of lavender and bacon
I contemplate.

I haven't quite gotten it yet.

Everything

Cheek to cheek caravan.
Careless love.
Do it again deep in a dream.

Cast your shadows.
Cast your fate.
Cast your bird chasings.

Optimistic and cock-eyed.
Your cold heart pours cocktails for two.
I drink to a gluttoned clarinet marmalade.

Come dance with me.
Come fly with me.
Dizzy and down with love.

Everything I have is yours.
I have everything but you.

High Heart

It's always there,
anyplace I hang my heart,
even these so many miles high.

After you, who?
Baby its cold outside tonight.
Won't you come home?
How 'bout some inventive decency.

I'm sitting here nailed to the process.
       Burning.
       Burnt.
       Burnt.
       Burnt.
            It's all burning.

Hidden in a tiny room
between somewhere and nowhere.
Black coffee and fallen blossoms.
Baby, you got me with the blues.
       Blue.
       Blue.
       Blue.
            Burnt and blue.

Mechanism

Entombed within these 4 walls
waiting on the mechanism to expose itself,
I get up to straighten a picture on the wall
for the third time.
Crooked right.
Then left.
Then right again.
I give up and accept its crooked nature.

I enjoy days like this.
These cavernous lurkings.
Hoping to be inspired by anything or everything.
And if it doesn't come today that's ok too.
It's enough to just enjoy
the Grand River crossing's caged breeze.

When the force inevitably awakens itself
I will reach mountaintops at Sunapee
swallowing the sounds of black velvet
in the invisible equinox.
On fire.

Sparse

Like a counter piece to my ballad.
Every time we say goodbye I'm strangely satisfied.
Moments full of promise evaporate
and mockingbirds sneer broad sneers.
Not seeming false.
And she crosses her legs one last time
making it impossible to leave.
She has infiltrated my marrow,
holding a vigil to endure.
Strangling me with raw avocado flesh.

No way to outwit love.
It's so rare and brutal.
Perfectly skyward.

We are witness to the sparse and limitless.

Sinister Samplings

Picking my nose and wiping the outcome
on the underside of my office chair,
I realize diamonds can be imitated,
but these are sinister samplings
leaving no room for disorder.

Perfection disgusts me.
It's an illusion of course.
Like picking tomatoes and feeling liberated.
Or a killer feeling guilty.
Or a drunk feeling sober.

Kidney stones and urinary tracts
and dangling hoop earrings.
Now that's real!

So are butterflies hell bent and sideways.
I prefer what's real of course.
I beg for what's real.

And I regret it when I get it.

Mood Mellow

There is an eternal triangulation
as the echoes of Harlem wail.
Easy living.
Exactly like you.
Four or five times the freight train's haul.
For all we know the forest flower is a flat flamingo.

It's mellow.
The mood is mellow today.
Here's to young lovers.
And heat waves too.
Here's to hot honeysuckle blues.
And hundred-year rains too.

Happiness is a thing called hooray.
Has anyone seen the nocturnal sun?
Has anyone else ever felt that way?

As It Is

The water evaporates
as is its course
and the creatures of the earth live only to die.
The mountains rise and the mountains fall
as is their course
and the living things of the earth await our fate.

The stars are formed and then destroyed
in the name of creation
 as is their course
and you and me and him and her,
we all kill time as time is killing us
and it's all as it should be.

It's all as it is.
It's all as it ever was.
It's all as it ever will be.

Shining

We sway toward the evening cool in our own sweet way,
heavy with a mist not yet sentimental.
Isn't love a reaching thing most universal?
Seeing you in the shadow of the moon
never to smile again
so perfect is perfection.
I surrender.

And do you remember the waterfront?
Kennebunkport.
Lazy and lush.
You danced for me that night.
You danced like lilacs in the rain.
And we made sweet love on the beach that night.
With sand and passion as our blanket.
We found magic at midnight that night.

My shining romance.
My shining hour.

Nothing Lasts

Going through the thing real quiet.
Characteristic immoderation
associated with escape
on roads leading west.

Perhaps we never were.
Perhaps we aren't now.

Take these steps into the wild with me.
Nothing is made to last, you see?
Let's get our money's worth while we're here.
Let's get it while we can.

Is It So?

An occasional chance to feel strong
is like trying to juggle blood and fire
while the melting icicles drip and the rivers run uphill.

There is a morning dance, maybe you'll be there?
For the ships to pass silent on the streets
you must never let go of your loose grip.

If the sky is colored orange.
If it's mid-morning in May.
If the organ grinder's bop is swinging hard.
If there is buttermilk on the Alamo.
Then it is so.

Sunsets and Rainchecks

I peeled her a grape and it wasn't enough.
Prisoners of love, we must all tuck our dreams away.
　　　With flowers.
　　　And passions.
　　　And serenades.
　　　　　And red sails.
　　　　　And sunsets.
　　　　　And rainchecks.
So what?
Send in the clowns with a sugar foot song
to tell of how somebody stole my gal.

I've rented a small room at the lull hotel
where it's ten cents a dance
if you want to take the chance.

You know the place.
It's where everyone's tears flow like wine.

Most Perfect Peril

Time is hanging precariously as it always has.
     I did seek.
     I did find.
The failing 200,000-year experiment of humankind
carries on heavy and thick.

A chance spark.
A chance evolution.
An unlucky flaw.

93 million miles from the sun
we dimwittedly float through space time on a rock
worrying about who's fucking who.
And who ate the last Oreo.
And who left the toilet seat up.
And who was late clocking in at work.

It makes no sense yet makes perfect sense
as we are left in this most perfect peril.

Vain Some Time Ago

Feeling better and needing no reason for it
is a fine way to be
as some cat in some dark alley in some dank place
nibbles from a Chinese food to go container
and has never been happier.

So many secrets lie beyond me
and I make sure not to spoil the magic.
And I couldn't if I tried
so I settle with that and scratch my head
directly in the spot where my hair is thinning the most
to remind myself of how vain I once was
some time ago.

Grey

The grey areas are more easily understood
when we're older and dying of thirst,
burnt out like sons of bitches and cigarette ash
and fleshy launches of chances seldom and slim.

An overheard eulogy at a bus stop
recounts an insignificant life lived in a well-lighted place
that could have been mine or could have been yours.
        But it wasn't mine.
        And it wasn't yours.
        It was only his.

He the loner genius.
He forever young.
I guess he will never know the grey areas
as I now do.

Now Moments

Regrets are grinding and looming large
in an instant near the fear.
Near the trembling.
Studying the handful of murderous now moments.
Forgetful of the rest.
I've been trying to save some tiny piece of anything
roaring within.
Sentimental again.

An Alan Watts electric passage,
buried tame and unweaving.
A category of being exotic like wildfires.

She had helped me overcome the commonness
of the days and nights.
The painless Parisian suicides.
Quite curious incidents for the fish in the bowls.
The birds in the cages.
The dogs in the crates.

Finesse should be our last resort.

The Word Forms

Again duped and derailed by all the gritty bottoms,
I'm leaning on invent to re-awaken
the dried-up discoveries.

      Finding the time.
      Forming the words.

The need to create has been there
as long as I can remember.
It's so easy to get lost in the sloppy shuffle.
Guts splashed all over the pages
like picking up porcupines
with bare hands,
joyous and wild.

Dry tongued desperation.

Writing is the world's greatest tonic.
The grand venture sum.

With flowing soul juices,
I'm whacking vultures with fly swatters
and still able to puke in stride.

I'm giving them the best damn show in town!

Hardly a Task

The tough times are meant to be remembered
I suppose.

Not dwelled upon.
Just revisited gently now and again.

The reality and the delusion.
Minds torn to tatters
and lapping up the sad flavors of regret
and misery and insanity.

I now find myself thirsty for them somehow.
Hungry for the fight.
Those days seem distances ago now.
Those wildfires laughing through the flames
beneath and beyond the blue hills and the blue earth.
Even the blue clouds were witness
when death was hardly a task.

But on the other side of this good fire
lay many bright waters within the mermaid tides.

I lay here considering the illumination
of those many distanced battlefields
no longer waging war much.

I know it was luck then.
As I know it's luck now.

Masterpiece

Time to toss out the tender and the two-bit
and go to war with the rest.
It's the words.
It's the fire.
It's the poems.

Yeah, the poems allow me to face the impossible
and fight where others choose to quit.
Right up to the grave's edge.
It's an instinctive thing.
Luckily, I was never taught.

Writing from a position of the self-created
is power itself.
Raw power.
True power.
Like madness with a comical lining.
Laughing at death.
Laughing at life.
Laughing at all things in between.

Misunderstood,
the champions continue to go unnoticed.

Ends and Beginnings

Screams so rarely reach their mark
with gossamer strands and Elysian strongholds,
poked to pieces and making a mess of the dollhouse.

How can one scream when no mouth remains?

I was told there'd be plenty of agony to go around.
Enough to make sure comfort can't get its foothold
in the swamp where bitter frogs fail to croak tender on pads.

Getting older has some benefits
and death is only one of them.
Gnawing at the despoiling of my own hard-boiled life,
I realize that the end of things
usually beats the beginnings.

Wait for the Silence

Babbling ripples of unnecessary chatter.
I've never understood people
who need to talk about their day at work
when they get home from work.

I'm the type that never wanted to go to work
In the first place.
Why the hell would I want to discuss it
after I'm finally freed from the noose for a few hours?

The way I see it t
hey already have us by the throat and balls
so why give them the tongue too,
why cough up the day's occurrences
just to relive it all over again.

And if you have a wife you can forget about escaping it.
You better smile while she's feeding you her trivialities
and don't you dare get caught daydreaming on her.

The older I've become
more still my tongue has become.

I just listen, nod and smile occasionally
while waiting for the silence to echo.

Dwellings

Imbibing from the well of authenticity,
somehow I'm going to let the others
concern themselves with my soul.
Inhaling these quiet walls I am an excellent fool.
A perfect fool.
A genius fool, really.
They will appreciate it one day.
Or not.
No matter, really.

Until then I will dwell in the places
where good gets better and better gets poisoned.
And open wounds fester.
And bubble.
And ooze undiscovered greatness.

I'm a late entrant to a party
I didn't even intend to attend.

Way Down

I drink alone after you've gone,
the lowest of my breed harboring unclean feelings
like the high waters on Beale Street
or bad luck in back alleys.
Its early morning somewhere
and the driving rain is moaning
like nobody knows its pain.
But I do.

And I think when you came over here tonight
you had trouble in mind.
And baby I followed you right on down.
You shook me good
and spoon fed me your sugar, fine and mellow.
Then hung it up quick like a long-distance phone call.

Now I'm way down and gin soaked.
Full of tear drops and too bad.
The only trouble with women
is when they come and when they go.

Gripping the Rareness

Throwing words in the air like confetti.
Not trying to work too hard.
Feeling the dull, dull, dullness
of being the hydrant pissed on by the dog.
Thread bare and brittle.
The wasting of wait.
Stirring up the juice gushing's
to splash against tricky ways
and fill these pages with a painter's eye
and a simplicity set on fire.
      Hot.
      Singing.
      Sizzling.

After days and weeks of falling apart,
fed upon by damnable urges and utter inconveniences,
I'm feeling a clipped and explosive craving
coming into me and over me.
Gripping the rareness dark and steady.
Grabbing the fire by the flame.

Into the Easy Roll

The mornings appeal to me.
They have since youth.
But arising early today
I'm stuck in the starting gate, refusing to move,
thinking of first moments and final moments
and all those in between.
What a ride!

I've covered every inch of wall space
and that's still worth something.
Arriving at the game later than most,
with nerve and durability and sensibilities
constantly bothered by the heads buried in sand,
I am feeling my way through each movement
not wanting to play the safe coward.

I want to swallow the olive with the martini.
I want wonder-filled chills of the breakaway.
I want sleep deprived, muse dependent,
one winged flight patterns.
The material is everywhere.
In everything I see.
To be dead before death is the only fear left.
I'm easing deeper than ever into the easy roll of it all.

Light Wading

Go to bed satisfied.
Wake up starving like a madman turned loose.
Letting the words speak for themselves
is chancing it, with a clenched fistful of light
wading in the murk.

So many years spent sitting on the crapper.
Elbow rested on knee.
Rubbing my temples.
Rubbing my eyes.
Thinking of all the dirty tricks played against a man.
The time spent worrying about people
who don't worry about me.
Always right in the middle and at a distance still.
Only wanting the next, not the last.
Borrowing reasons.
Knowing that late beginners must never stop pounding.
Or else.

Hiding Place

I'm trying to remain buoyant in these poetic oceans.
Surviving one struggle just to face another.
Very much knowing that the voiceless pendulum
is the best option of many bad options.
There have been plenty of poems in each bottle.
Preferring the rough to the smooth.
Observing the mysterious source of creation
with its routes and roulette balls
and funeral processions.

I figure I'm not bad for a college dropout
chewing at mind frames and viewpoints
and non-standard forms.
Refusing to swallow the bait so obvious.

I should have died from being pent up
in all those ways.
Not a pretty way to go.
But I took the drab and flailing, ponderous hollow
empty bottom parts and turned them into truth.
Valid so.
And I have become a small-time writer of no acclaim,
sick with a feverish need to feed upon unscrambled,
simple notes of language.

It's my last hiding place.

Performers

Shaking life into a glorious gut ripped verve,
I'm throttling the tickle of the fake dream.
Our nights are numbered from birth
... but who's counting?

The luckiest things seem the hardest to gauge
because one man's rantings
won't always be another man's ravings.

The moon seems to be darkening a bit tonight
but the evening is bright still
as the circus performers and carnival types
are all milling about.
A woman with a beard approaches
and tells me a bear has stolen her picnic basket.

Such flashing strange signals it all is.
An illumination of yes?
The music has never sounded so good.
So real.
So full.

What a candy-striped affair this whole thing is.
A little man, standing next to a very tall man,
standing next to a very strong man,
pulls his glasses down his nose,
 right to the tip and is staring at me.
Then he says, "jazz is the new classical, man."

I smile at him.
I believe he is correct.

Too Clean to Burn

Laughing by myself.
Words floating around such long shadows
cast by the great ones.

It could have happened at the Village Vanguard.
It could have happened if I sat at the front table
while Coltrane was searching.

No.
That's too clean.
Too neat.
Let's burn it.
Not all the way down.
Just part way.
It will burn in impossibility.
It will burn in proper dosages.

The whole scheme
relies on the beautifully worked nothing moments,
but the nights are running short for me now
and the stench of ugliness is left dangling.
Trane knew the old thrill.

These must be the days of vanishing originalities.

Dissipation

Wage slaved down into the sick early morning half dark,
we keep on accepting the bad things
Proud of our dirt.
With the lost edges of a slow driving breakthrough.
What a flea spotted
and unsavory dissipation of the dream we have accepted.
Smashed up against the rocks, limp and dismal,
I'm bent over lacing my boots.

I'm an old timer playing it loose
amidst the shadowy and subnormal.

I've never lacked potential.
I've just rarely reach it.

Shelled Remains

The anchors are up on the purist form
as it becomes the other thing,
and I'm peering out a 12th floor window
not wanting to look down
into the vacuum of returns diminished.

There is a piercing, double-barreled,
 double fisted uneasiness in my stomach
that I veil with canned laughter,
but the child still wakes up screaming
and my interest rates are still in the high twenties.

My tattered nerves have long since decayed
and my eyes remain pain filled,
viewing birds, fat and fleshy, at the feeder
and I am the shelled remains on the ground.

Weighed Down

My mind, dismissive and impotent with drink,
begins feeling weighed down by a carved sense of futility,
while pathetic and inadequate words are masquerading
as profound blunt pencil scrawls.

But we know better, don't we?

Drinking less than I used to,
but more than I should,
I never know if the car is going to start.

I should have never switched from white lined paper
to yellow lined paper.

What a dangerous signal that was.

Awoke

If its war a man is after he will surely find one.
Or many more than one.
If its peace a man is after
he will surely find none lasting.
Wars rage on.
Hatred rages on.
And that's fine.
It's been that way since the beginning it seems.

Man craves power.
Man craves money.
Man craves ownership
of things never meant to be owned.

Man is the weakest creature there is.
Ever was.
Man wasn't meant to last too long.
And that's fine.
Just long enough for a few great ones to awaken.
And they have over time.

But the master has an illness now.
And a cure doesn't exist.
So our time is soon up.
Our days are numbered.
Yet somehow I awoke
feeling very much alive today.
More alive than I've ever felt perhaps.
And that's more than enough for me.

Old Things

Scribbling lines of distinction on stolen stationary.
Turning pages into poems immortal.
I couldn't possibly dial it back!
Not at the pawn shop.
Not at the funeral parlor.
Not while drinking homemade sangria.

It seems even the fireflies
are wishing me good fortune these days.
And I can smell the ease of the flowers
while walking on thunder so blue.
So roaring.
Bleeding the sky.
It's a twisted and luminous walk.
Never ending and nailed to the paper.
The old thing suddenly made new.
The old thing reborn and eternal.

Withheld Screams

She'd been haunting me all morning,
speaking gently of her life battles,
tip toeing around trying not to wake the kid.
She had become disoriented
by the freedom of things too well adjusted.
She preferred the primal and the marginal.
The quick swings.
It was all beginning to slip.
Gone was the strut of the alligator.
No more jumping out of moving cars.
It was all books on tape
and claustrophobic window watching now.

But this morning she was locked back in.
Hitting the handle jug early and often.
This is what happens when withheld screams explode.
What happened next seemed odd at the time
but now I get it.
She felt her artwork was getting weak and floppy.
Lacking truth.
I probably wouldn't have thought to piss on the paintings
like that.
The way she did.

I'm just not that cool, I guess.

Far Too Sensitive

I told her I've been drinking through the sunsets
and sleeping with my clothes on.
I stay open to the dream
like pirates and buried treasure
and enjoying views, as minutes fold
 and hours carry heavy treads
on street corners of another kind.

I know there's a flow to it.
I know poems can have punchlines.
I know there are honest moments
and sure ways to do things.

But I also know about damaged sorts
and the new thing, free.
I told her all these things
and her response was, *"typical you."*

She always did say I was far too sensitive
for my own good.

Don't Bet Against the House

There is always a profound humor to be found
in the heavy setting juice of it all,
seeping in and at the ready.
It's our job to find the potentiality of it,
these so many degrees of wild-eyed insanity.
Better to laugh than cry?
Sure.
Even the monks are dancing these days.

Somewhere, right now, a frog is clearing his throat
while a sex starved husband is weighing his options.
Unblinking raw forms of agonies and entanglements,
slow and incurable, are laughing
in the face of insurmountable odds.

With all the distractions on-going and often,
it's easy to forget that the house always wins.

Last Dance

These words are scribbled
        in hopes of rupturing the mundane, you see,
        the divide is great and final wisdoms
        are held together by misunderstandings.
For all the forgotten injustices.
For all the slobbery dullness.
For all the self-congratulatory sweethearts.
For all the dogs pooping out stolen socks.
For all the ruined teeth.
For all the gold teeth.
For all the conveyor belts and logical solutions.
For all the quick suicides and those lasting a lifetime.
For all the abortive attempts and abstract truths.
For all the refined actors playing the part
        and instinctive natures as well.
For all the impending tragedies and forgettable heroes.
For all the trolls living under bridges.
For each of these.
And for me.
And for you.

There will always be a last dance
which can only be danced alone.